Beauty in the Beast

Publication Date: November 18, 2019

ISBN-13: 978-1-7750252-9-0

 ~ ~

Daria stumbled through the dark forest. She'd lost track of the path she'd been on, she was sure of it. What if she was entering the territory of the Beast that was rumoured to live in these woods?

The air trembled with a roll of thunder. And now a storm was coming. She could catch her death of cold, or even get hit by lightning!

Maybe she shouldn't have left her town behind. But she'd had no choice. Gustav wouldn't take no for an answer—even after she'd finally worked up the nerve to try to tell him so. It wasn't a woman's place to make such objections.

Lightning flashed. A tall figure barred her way, an axe on his shoulder. Daria stopped short with a gasp, stepping back.

"What are you doing on my land?" the man growled.

"I...didn't know it was yours," Daria stuttered in a small voice. "I just...got lost, and now it's dark and cold..." Thunder rumbled again in the distance.

He stared at her for another expressionless moment. "Come with me." He turned away.

Released from his intense gaze, Daria let out a breath. At least he wasn't dragging her off. But she couldn't bring herself to move. *What if he's the Beast?* Did she dare to go with him? Did she dare not to, and risk incurring his wrath? She didn't want to be left behind either, not when it meant being caught in the rain. She hastened to follow him before he went out of sight.

As they passed into the even deeper blackness beneath the trees, the man stooped to gather up a bundle of chopped logs under one arm. Daria felt some measure of relief. Of course. That was why he was out here in the forest with an axe; he had simply been cutting firewood with it.

But that didn't mean he couldn't still use it for other purposes.

The man continued leading the way through the evergreens. Daria rubbed her hands up and down her arms. The long sleeves did little to fight the chill. She had to avoid the jutting branches of the barren trees, but their poking tips often scraped or caught on her clothes anyway. It was so dark that sometimes she only had the sounds of the man's passage ahead of her to go by.

Soon they emerged onto a narrow dirt path, which wound halfway up the slope before them to a large building that loomed against the night sky. Another lightningbolt revealed it to be a decrepit residence with greyed plank walls, its steep shingle roof harbouring a single turret. It looked just like the cursed manse of lore. Where the Beast took his victims.

With every step up the incline, Daria felt a greater tightness banding her chest. Why was she doing this? She could be walking right into a deathtrap!

But she forced herself to calm down. She knew better than to put too much stock in hearsay. There could be any number of men living out here in remote cabins. Besides, if the man meant her harm, why hadn't he acted on it already? He hadn't even looked over his shoulder to see if she was following.

They went up a few steps onto a roofed porch, lined with square wooden columns, to enter through a weathered side door.

The interior was just as bare and lifeless. Dust coated the faded floorboards, and the air smelled stale. Grey sheets were draped over a few high piles of irregular shape.

The man sent the door swinging

closed behind Daria. He crossed to a dormant hearth on the other side of the room and deposited the logs onto the floor beside it, leaning his axe against the wall. He squatted before the fireplace and set some wood inside.

He eyed her over his shoulder, then took something out of his inside coat pocket. He touched the object to the logs, and they caught alight immediately. Surprised, Daria craned her neck to try to see it better. How had he done that? There had been no strike of flint on steel. But he tucked the thing away again and rose, taking his axe with him as he went through a left-hand archway ahead.

The sky lit up one more time, and then the patter of rain started on the windowpanes, growing louder until it was a constant drumming. Daria was briefly grateful she hadn't been caught out in it after all, but the feeling soon withered under her apprehension of being inside this forbidding residence.

She waited, but when the man didn't return, her eyes drifted to the light of the hearth. The warmth of the blaze drew her closer, and she came to a stop a few feet before it, holding her hands out to the heat.

The looming shadow of the man reentered, and Daria took an involuntary step back, withdrawing her hands.

He pointed at the high-backed armchair facing the fireplace. "Sit."

Watching him, she hesitantly backed into it, hands on the armrests as she lowered herself onto the seat.

He came to stand beside the mantelpiece, and folded one arm atop it. He fixed Daria with his stern gaze. "What brings you into the middle of the woods, at night, alone?"

With a discomfited twinge, she dropped her eyes, fingering the stitching on her skirt. "I...left Nordham. This morning. There's nothing for me there." She sighed. "I guess I didn't give much thought to where I was going, as long as it was away."

The man watched her in silence. The ruddy glow from the fire cast his long angular face in stark shadow. Then he looked out the rain-streaked window, the ragged ends of his lank black hair brushing his shoulders. "There's no settlement for miles." He returned his gaze to the mantel. "The other rooms aren't any more accommodating than this one, so you'll have no need to enter them."

Daria studied him. Was he offering to let her stay for the night? Before she accepted any hospitality, however grudgingly alluded to, she had to know who he was. He could be intending to confine her to this room whether she wanted it or not. "Are you...the one they call...the Beast?"

He looked over at her with a dark, silent glance.

She went on hastily, "It's just...you don't look the part, and...this doesn't seem like very beastly behaviour."

His expression seemed a bit placated.

"They call me that, yes," he admitted levelly. "But it is undeserved."

Daria's mind brimmed with curiosity. Then how much of the stories applied to him? She was tentative in voicing her thoughts. "They say you're as wild as the wolves, and that you...prey on whoever crosses your path."

He pressed his mouth into a thin line. "I don't perpetrate violence," he said quietly.

"Then...all those rumours...?"

His eye glinted. "Purely folktales."

Daria knew that every fable had a kernel of truth, though. "What made them invent such things about you?"

"Anything mysterious or unexplained is fodder for superstition. They don't understand why I live in a run-down shack in the middle of the woods."

"Why do you?"

He regarded her for a moment. "It was once my family's estate. It was abandoned many years ago, and has since fallen into disrepair. I have returned, to attempt to restore it."

Daria found herself relaxing a little. The nearby flames had warmed this nook of the chilly house, enough to start thawing her to the bone. "And nobody's ever come up here to greet you?"

He shook his head. "Never bothered. They don't even seem to realize I have a name."

Daria watched him, attentive. "Then what might it be?" she asked gently.

He eyed her sidelong before responding. "Geordon."

Nothing monstrous about that. She offered a small smile. "Mine's Daria."

He looked away before long, and straightened off the mantel, shifting one foot. "It's late," he said, changing the subject. "Do you need to eat?"

"No. But thank you," she murmured. "I brought some rations with me." She'd had enough forethought for that, at least. She still had some provisions in the pouch at her hip, but only enough for another small meal.

Geordon nodded. "Settle in. I'll be upstairs." He turned and went back out through the archway.

In spite of herself, Daria looked over her shoulder at the door. If she still needed to get away, this might be her one chance, now that he was gone. But the downpour was still pelting out there. And besides, he *had* provided ample cause to believe he wasn't the Beast he was said to be, or any such thing. She tucked her feet up under her on the seat, and leaned one elbow on the armrest. *He's just a man, as normal as any other,* she told herself.

She still eyed the shadowy corners of the room with some unease, and twitched when the walls creaked from a stiff gust of wind. She wasn't sure she could get any rest in this unfamiliar place.

But eventually, the beat of the rain on the walls began to lull her, along with the warmth of the fire. Under the drowsy weight of the late hour, she lowered her head onto her folded arm, watching the mesmerizing flames until her eyes slowly slid closed.

Daria stirred, lifting her head—and started when the first thing she saw was Geordon. He was watching her from beside the right-hand archway, leaning against the wall with his arms folded. Daria levered herself upright in the armchair, rather self-conscious. How long had he been there?

The morning sky out the window was white with clouds, and the rain was long gone. The fire had also dwindled to embers.

"Got enough sleep?" Geordon prompted.

"Uh...I suppose so." She briefly sank her fingers in her brown hair, shifting where the tapering tips lay just past her shoulders.

Geordon headed to the other side of the room, and Daria watched him around the corner of the backrest, then got up from her seat.

"Urdstrom is five hours southeast of here," he said.

Daria drifted after him, at a bit of a loss as to what he was talking about.

"A path at the bottom of the hill leads there." He turned back to her and opened the door.

She gazed at the view beyond. "You're...letting me leave?" She lifted her eyes to his. "Even after you told me your secrets?"

Geordon smiled faintly. "The truth is no worse than rumour." He gestured with one hand. "You're free to go."

Slowly, Daria stepped outside, but paused just past the threshold, eyes on the porch. "I..." She turned to look back at him. "I don't know anyone there," she murmured. "I don't have enough money for room and board, let alone a new place to live." Her gaze drifted down again in despondence, as she realized the extent of the predicament she was in. She hadn't fully considered how much it would take to start over.

Geordon glanced to the side. "You can stay here," he said, and Daria met his eyes, feeling some surprised hope. "At least until you decide what to do."

Even so, she was still hesitant. Taking shelter from a storm for a single night was one thing, but taking up longer residence with a strange man she barely knew...

Geordon's mouth quirked. "It's not much of a place, but at least you're welcome to it."

Daria's heart was touched with gratitude. Despite his curt manner, he kept offering to help her at every turn. Definitely not the actions of a Beast. He was more of a gentleman than many men she knew, in his own rugged way. "That's very generous."

Geordon simply gave a grunt, and

spread an arm back toward the inside of the house.

After they reentered, Geordon prepared a meal of porridge and bread in the kitchen, though he left Daria to eat hers alone in the armchair before the dark hearth. Afterwards, Geordon gave her a flint and steel to light the fire with—clearly not whatever he'd used last night. When that didn't take much time, he even found her a leatherbound book to settle down with by the fireside—but it was such a dry read, she couldn't concentrate on it for long.

Throughout the day, he always seemed to be lurking around, as if to make sure she didn't get up to anything. He showed up especially whenever she wandered near one of the archways to the front room, blocking her way, often ready with some new remark or suggestion of a pastime for her. Daria squinted past him, but there was nothing noteworthy about the dim parlour beyond. What was he trying to hide?

Finally, when dusk fell, Geordon told her that she could stay in a room upstairs. He led the way into the dark parlour with its ceiling twenty feet above. A ledge ran around the three far walls, lined with sculpted wooden columns and railings on all but the side closest to the front double-doors. Atop stood several items and small pieces of furniture, which looked quite out of place and precarious up there. There were also more heaps of objects on the floor, some of them peeking out from underneath the sheets. Daria tried to get a look at them in passing.

Geordon eyed her sidelong. "Don't touch anything," he warned.

They went up a few steps onto the raised stage covering the far half of the room, then climbed the grand staircase to the colonnade. At the end of the hall, Geordon opened a worn door. The room beyond was wide and furnished with a few more large shapes covered by grey sheets. Three tall windows, framed by diaphanous curtains that stirred in the indoor drafts, were spaced out across the wall ahead, looking south. A low, rickety cot stood in the rough middle of the floor, with several layers of dusty blankets serving for a mattress.

"This is the best there is," Geordon said.

Daria wondered if she wouldn't rather sleep on the armchair again anyway. But she couldn't very well turn down the chance to have a room to herself. "It's enough," she replied instead.

"There's firewood beside the hearth," he said. When she nodded, Geordon turned away and pulled the door closed on his way out.

A second later, a click came from it. Frowning, Daria crossed to it, and tried the knob. The door wouldn't budge. She rattled the knob, tugging on the door in desperation. He'd locked her in! Maybe this had all been a ruse to keep her captive here after all. Just when she started thinking she could trust him, he did something like this!

Finally, she gave up the effort, and tried to reassure herself. It didn't mean he had ominous intentions for her. Maybe he was just paranoid, and didn't want her wandering around his house in the night. Daria turned back to the room, but there were no other ways out. The windows were too high up to climb out of, and they didn't even open.

Her eyes fell on the blanket-draped heaps. She was still immensely curious as to what was really underneath them. And if she was going to be sequestered in here anyway, she might as well have a look. If Geordon didn't want her to, he shouldn't have put her in the same room with them. She went over to one, and lifted a corner of the dark grey sheet to peek behind it. All she saw were some old chairs and end tables piled up together. She checked all the other ones, but it was nothing but more furniture. She sat on the edge of the cot in disappointment. Of course he'd only put her in a room that had no secrets to uncover.

The next morning, Daria stood rubbing the small of her stiff back with one hand, when the doorknob jiggled. She looked at it, then drifted closer. A minute later, a key turned in the lock, and Geordon opened the door.

He met her eyes. "Sorry, this faulty old door locks sometimes when it's closed."

Glad understanding swept through Daria. A grain of doubt remained, though, as to whether he was just contriving that story. But why else would he have tried to open the door before going to get the key?

Her final piece of certainty was

restored when he handed her the key. "In case it happens again."

Daria looked down at it in her palm. She should really stop thinking the worst of him, when time and again it turned out to be nothing but a misunderstanding.

Geordon half-turned back to the doorway. "Want to go for a walk?" She glanced up at him in surprise. "For some fresh air."

It *would* be good to stretch her legs, after being cooped up in this room all night. Daria tucked the key into her belt pouch, and nodded.

They headed downstairs and went out the same side door, then proceeded down the porch steps and onto the pale dirt of the path. Everything had dried up after the rainstorm of two nights ago, but the low overcast remained. The sparse grass that covered the ground was dead and matted, a dull yellow-brown that matched the rest of the drab landscape.

Geordon gestured to the eastward lane. "That leads to the farther town of Rodendard." He walked the other way, and Daria accompanied him. He looked down the sloping path on their left, which looped around to become the one they had first taken up to the house. At the foot of the hill it split, veering southeast. "That way's Urdstrom."

Daria looked at him, wondering if he was listing her options.

As they kept onward, they neared a crossroad, beyond which, the course they were on continued west. "And that's back to Nordham."

She drifted to a stop. "I'd rather not be heading closer to that place."

Geordon glanced at her. Then he tilted his head toward the trail that crossed in front of the manor to rise north up the hillside. "That one goes to the dam. If you don't mind a bit of an uphill climb."

The bushes nearby rustled, and a

timber wolf emerged. Daria gasped, shying back, as it was followed by a whole pack that came trotting toward them.

"Don't fear," Geordon reassured her, setting a hand on one wolf's fur. The others circled around them, more like curious dogs than predators. "They won't hurt you, not if you're with me."

She watched them with wide eyes. "So you really can speak to the animals," she breathed.

Geordon lifted the corner of his mouth wryly. "Not in so many words," he demurred. "We just understand each other."

A wolf nosed at Daria's skirt. With her arms tucked up before her, she kept her hands to herself, and resisted the urge to pull away.

"You can give them a pat, if you like," Geordon told her.

Daria considered extending a tentative hand onto the wolf's head—but then decided that was too close to its jaws, and it would be all too easy for it to bite her hand off. The wolf lowered its snout to the ground and turned partly away, but still stood close to her. Very cautiously, Daria reached down and lightly sank her fingers into the brownish-grey fur on the wolf's back. It was coarse, but thick and warm. The wolf's shoulder shifted, and Daria whisked her hand back.

The wolf wandered over to the others, and several of them started tussling and playing together. Without the element of danger, Daria began to feel a sort of appreciative wonder. She'd never seen a wolf up-close. She hadn't thought she'd wanted to, before.

Geordon started up the northward path, and Daria hastened to keep pace. Some of the wolves swung about to jog along with them, tongues lolling. They frequently loped off into the woods, only to rejoin them later. Daria eyed them uneasily, finding it stressful to try to keep track of where they all were.

"Would you prefer if they didn't

accompany us?" Geordon prompted her. Evidently, the expression on her face was answer enough. He turned to the wolves. "All right, gang, as you were." They all regrouped and lolloped off into the forest.

Daria stared after them. "Do they always do what you tell them?"

"They'll do as I ask, because they decide to," he qualified. "I don't control them."

That was a bit of a comfort. The only people she'd heard of—in stories, anyway—who were capable of commanding animals were evil witches or necromancers.

The two of them continued up the incline. The still air was crisp, but the exercise kept her warm enough.

"You can come out here whenever you want," Geordon told her. "You're not obliged to stay inside."

Daria looked over at him. The way he said it made her wonder if he'd prefer her to be out of the house, so he wouldn't have to keep an eye on her, like he had yesterday.

She returned her gaze to the ground. It might be nice to have the freedom to roam the grounds at leisure—but then again, she wasn't sure she'd want to be out here on her own when there were wolves roving about. Geordon had only said they wouldn't harm her *if* she was in his company.

A dark shape moved in the woods ahead, and Daria looked up. A big black bear had risen onto its hind legs, and was watching them.

Her breath caught and her step faltered. She glanced at Geordon, but he didn't seem the least bit concerned, so she kept walking, keeping her eyes on the bear. At least she had Geordon between her and it.

The bear dropped to all fours again, and started ambling over to them.

"He a friend of yours too?" Daria prompted Geordon, in a voice that was a bit too tenuous to be casual.

He smiled faintly. As the bear joined

his side, Geordon briefly ruffled a fond hand on its head. "They all are."

Daria studied Geordon with a trace of impressed admiration. If he could tame the wild beasts with just his presence, there must be something about him that was gentler than the average man.

~ ---- ~

That evening, the two of them sat before the fireplace in the side room. Geordon had pulled up a chair, obtained from one of the blanketed piles.

"You really don't want to return to Nordham?" he asked Daria gently. "What made you leave?"

Her eyes were downcast. "I have no family to stay for. The people there are so...uncaring, so spiteful. They make the place even more bleak than it already is. And there's this one man, Gustav, who fancied himself my suitor. He was determined to make me his wife, and I'd have little say in the matter. With no father or brothers to speak on my behalf, none of the villagers would interfere. But I could never marry a man like that, who would only see me as the token of another successful hunt."

Geordon studied the floorboards, as if trying to find the words. "You shouldn't have had to face that."

Daria looked up at him, poignantly moved by his compassion. No other man had been on her side about it. He was so different from Gustav. He expected nothing, demanded nothing. He just let her be who she was. She appreciated it more than she could say.

~  ~

Daria came down on the fourth morning to find Geordon loading more logs into the fireplace. As he headed away, she stood with her hand on the back of the armchair, gazing at the hearth. She remembered how he'd inexplicably kindled it before, without seeming to first strike a spark.

"Geordon..." she said, and he paused to look back at her. It was the first time she'd spoken his name. "Can I ask you something?"

His expression became a bit droll. "You've done so before."

She turned her eyes to him. "That thing you used to light the fire the first night...what was it?"

Geordon considered her for a long moment. Then he murmured, "Well, you already know everything else about me." He turned and went through the archway into the front room. When he came back, he held in his hands an object that looked like a brass oil lamp, but more compact. "It's a lamp of dragonfire. Its ever-flaming liquid will set fire to anything it's poured on."

Daria drew in a breath of awe. No wonder the logs had ignited so spontaneously.

"I collect magical artifacts like it, from all across the land. I brought them all back here, so they would have a safe and secluded place to stay. My family had several of their own, passed down as heirlooms. They're what first inspired me to become a collector."

She never imagined she'd encounter magic in her own lifetime! "There are other artifacts?" she prompted, eager to know more.

"Want to see them?" Geordon guessed. But then his gaze turned earnest and intent. "I trust you won't tell anyone else about this," he added.

"Not a soul!" she agreed readily. Who would she tell, anyway?

He studied her for another moment, then showed a bit of a smile and nodded. He went back into the parlour, and this time she followed. He flapped back the dark grey sheet on one heap, and carefully set the dragonfire lamp inside a stone chest behind. Of course; that must have been what he'd wanted to keep her from finding under the blanketed piles. Artifacts.

Then he beckoned her over to a stack of crates beneath the ledge and climbed them, pausing and turning back each step of the way to help her up. When their hands met, their eyes locked for a prolonged moment. It was the first time they'd actually touched. Daria hadn't expected his strong hand to be so gentle, or that she'd feel so comfortable with it. But then Geordon turned away again, and they soon made it to the top.

Sitting catacorner on the ledge was a narrow cupboard that came up to her shoulder height. It was painted powder blue, but was so scuffed and battered that nearly as much of it was white beneath the peeled and flaking coat as not.

"This is a teleportation cupboard," Geordon announced. "If you get in one and close the door, it transports you to the other one."

"This? But it looks so...ordinary."

"Most artifacts do. That's what makes them so hard to track down." Geordon set a hand on top of the cupboard. "Its twin stands in the turret on the third floor. The door to the turret was bricked over long ago, so this is the only way to get in and out of it." He regarded her sidelong. "Need a demonstration?"

"Well, it *would* be my first time seeing magic," she admitted.

"Feel free to take a look inside it after I

go—but make sure you close the door again, or I won't be able to get back here."

Daria looked at him questioningly.

"One door can only open if the other's closed," he explained. "That way, there can't be two people trying to teleport at the same time, and ending up occupying the same space."

She grimaced. She could imagine why they'd want to avoid that.

Opening the cupboard, Geordon crouched a little to step in, and pulled the door closed. A flash of blue light beamed through the cracks on either side. Daria snatched the door open again, but the interior was empty. She stared, then looked all around the inside. There was no false bottom, not when it stood on a ledge over the sitting room. She sidestepped to peek behind the cupboard, but there was no back door either. She came back in front and closed the door. A second later, it opened again, and Geordon stepped out, just as if he had been inside all along.

"Incredible," Daria murmured.

Geordon gave a small, teasing grin. "You want to try it?"

"Oh...I don't know..." she began dubiously. "I've never teleported before."

"You barely feel a thing. Other than a little disorentation when you get out," he added. "I'll go first, so I'll be waiting in the room when you get there." He climbed back in, and once he'd gone through, Daria took her turn at it.

She got into the cupboard, and after a hesitation made herself close the door. She stood there in the cramped dimness for a few moments, but nothing seemed to happen. Did it only work for Geordon? She opened the door and stepped out, but found herself in a small hexagonal room. Her mind swept a little.

Geordon stood before her, half-holding out a hand as if to steady her, a trace of a smile on his lips. "Weather your first trip all right?" he prompted.

Daria also felt a touch of vertigo, her body realizing she was a storey higher than she just had been. "I...think so." She studied the room until she got her bearings back. There were a lot of artifacts here too, but they were arrayed neatly on shelves around the walls, and carefully polished so they gleamed in the veiled midmorning sunlight from a small window. "What do the rest of these do?" she asked, heading over to them.

Geordon came up beside her, following her gaze to a round brass bauble, as big as a fist and carved with interlocking patterns. "That one comes right back to your hand after it hits what you throw it at. Handy in a fight." He went on to introduce the rest of them to her—from an inexhaustible cornucopia that provided Geordon with all the provisions he needed without ever having to go to town, where he might not be welcome—to a coil of grappling rope, which would wrap itself securely around anything it was tossed at—to an orb of levitation; a sphere of clouded crystal sized to fill the palm of the hand, which would let the holder float down safely from any height instead of falling. There was a master key that opened any lock there was, a compass that always pointed homeward, and a glove that could withstand the heat of a blast furnace, among dozens more.

Daria studied him. All this talk of artifacts brought out a vibrant aspect in him that made him seem five years younger—more like her age. Though she might be considered past her prime at twenty-five. It was quite in contrast to how grim he'd been at first. He clearly had a passion for what he did.

Daria found herself tempted to venture a playful comment. "Out of all these things, don't you have some sort of...magic hammer that restores buildings instantaneously?"

Geordon's mouth quirked. "Unfortunately, no. I've yet to find an artifact that convenient." His expression turned thoughtful. "I do have one that's quite the coincidence, though." He reached into his shirt and drew out a thin leather cord he wore around his neck, from which hung a silver medallion in the shape of a wolf's face. "This amplifies my connection to the animals across distances. Without it, we'd only be able to communicate if they were in my immediate presence. I was fortunate to find it. To anyone without the inherent bond, it would serve as nothing more than a trinket."

Daria watched him with wonder. "Are there others with abilities like yours? I mean, there must have been at some point, or there wouldn't be a medallion for it."

"It did give me validation that there have been other instances of it. But it's rare. I haven't found many accounts of it in history—but then again, it's not something that most would admit to being capable of." He tucked the medallion away.

Daria turned back to the objects on

display. "Do you ever use the rest of these?"

"Only when I have occasion to."

"Could it be that the possession of all these magical artifacts contributed to your reputation?"

Geordon cocked an eyebrow at her. "Yes, I'm sure it did. If anyone passing by saw them in action, that would add further to the unnerving mystique that others ascribe to me. I refrained from mentioning it as a reason before, since the existence of such priceless treasures is not something you share with a stranger."

Daria twisted her mouth wryly. She started strolling back along the shelves, looking over all the artifacts. "Can just anyone use them?"

"Yes. Most of them are simply activated by the touch of living skin, and then they do as they're made to, upon the wielder's will and direction." Geordon gave her a no-nonsense look. "But I don't advise that you toy with them on your own. You don't know how to wield all of them, and one misstep with something like the dragonfire lamp could burn the whole house down."

She made a face, both daunted and dissatisfied. "Point taken." She ran her fingers along the shelf, and tapped them in front of the cornucopia. "Shouldn't this be in the kitchen?" she wondered.

"It used to be," he admitted. "I moved it up here, along with a few other things that were laying about, after you arrived." Daria eyed him sidelong. "Didn't want you catching onto what they could do by accident."

When they teleported back into the parlour, Geordon took some of the artifacts with him, and returned them to their proper places. They had no secrets from each other anymore.

Daria did a lot of thinking the rest of that day, trying to figure out her next steps. She wouldn't want to overstay her welcome. But neither of her current options—return to her old town, or take her chances in a new one—were appealing. And, despite how run-down this place was, it was starting to grow on her. Most of Nordham wasn't in much better shape, and the company was worse. It seemed Geordon wasn't as gruff as he'd first let on, and she felt herself growing a certain esteem for him and his unique abilities. And where else would there be so many magical artifacts! It was to her own surprise that she found she didn't really want to leave, despite how eager she once might have been.

The following afternoon, Daria found Geordon outside, checking on a rain barrel off the side porch. Just seeing his face brought her heart an unexpected rise of warmth. Now that she knew his true character, what she'd once seen as severe features were now a welcome sight to her eyes. But then she dropped her gaze, not knowing what to do with these feelings. What she was about to say was likely presumptuous enough without bringing any such implications into it.

"Geordon," she began hesitantly, stepping up to him. "You said I could stay until I decided where to go, but..." She looked up at him. "My prospects aren't any better now than they were before." Her gaze drifted down to the side, then across the manor grounds. "I think...I want to stay here." She met Geordon's eyes. "This place feels more like home to me than anywhere I've been in a long time."

He looked upon her for a moment. "You're the only one I've trusted with all this." His voice was soft, too. "You've made this house much less lonely."

A tentative hope began to rise in Daria. Had he come to feel as much fondness for her as she did for him? She thought he'd simply tolerated her before, like an inconvenient interloper that was too nosy. But there was no mistaking the tenderness in his gaze now.

Geordon set a gentle hand on the side of her neck, and slowly stroked down it, running his palm around the front to rest on the skin below her collarbone. She could feel her heartbeat thumping against his hand. Then he withdrew it, still meeting her eyes.

As the days went on, Daria began lending a hand with the restoration efforts around the house, starting with uncovering some of the furniture, dusting it off, and moving it into the rooms where it belonged. She also carried planks and supplies to where they were needed for actual repairs, such as a leaky part of the roof in the attic, and held them in place while Geordon hammered. She managed to rustle up an old lumpy mattress that wasn't too musty, to use on her cot instead, and, in an antique wardrobe, she even found some decent dresses that she could launder and repurpose for herself.

But after a while, a worry began to nag at her. She hadn't told anyone in Nordham she was leaving. She was sure none of them cared—but it was only a matter of time before Gustav would notice she was gone. It might not have been right away, since he didn't come to court her every day. After all the time he'd spent on her, he wasn't likely to give up what he considered his rightful property. He might even think it the perfect opportunity to finally win her over, by 'rescuing' her from her captor in a blaze of heroic glory. And if he *was* on his way, Geordon had a right to know.

Daria brought it up when she saw him

next. "The man I told you about, Gustav—once he hears I went missing in your territory, he will come looking for me."

Geordon's brow creased with concern.

"He'll probably think I was captured by the Beast."

"And if he does?"

"I don't know what he'll do. He was already possessive and relentless in his pursuit of me. He might stop at nothing to get me back, even in the face of a Beast."

"Then I'll explain to him that you want to stay."

"He's not one to listen to reason. And he won't believe you, not when he still thinks you're the Beast." Daria was silent for a moment. "He could be dangerous."

"Do you think he would bring any villagers with him?"

She considered it, and twisted the corner of her mouth wryly. "No. They're too apathetic to be recruited to a cause just to get me back."

Geordon's expression became a little complacent. "If he comes alone, I can handle him."

Daria wondered if he was just putting on a show of confidence to reassure her. She knew he wouldn't actually fight Gustav if it came to that, since Geordon wasn't a proponent of violence. But she doubted Gustav had any such qualms. That's what worried her.

The day after, Daria was wiping dust off a dresser in the side room. When Geordon came back in with the firewood, his face held a troubled look. He met her eyes, and put his load down by the door. "The bear saw someone lurking in the area this morning. A pale-haired man with a sword."

Daria got a sinking feeling. It was as she'd feared. "Gustav," she breathed.

"I don't want you going out there," Geordon went on. "I'll send the wolves out to make sure he's not still around."

A few hours later, the pack reported

back that they hadn't come across Gustav. Geordon still had the animals stay on the lookout, and keep him apprised.

Daria was pacing in her room the next afternoon, lost in unsettled thought. She drifted over to the west window. She thought she glimpsed a figure at the treeline below, and her heart jumped. But when she looked again, no one was there. It hadn't been Geordon; he was still in the house. The fleeting sight had resembled Gustav. Maybe it was just her anxiety playing tricks on her.

She went straight downstairs and told Geordon.

His expression darkened. "How dare he come that close," he growled. "I'm going out there." He started for the front door.

"What about you?" she protested. "He has a sword."

"I have an axe," Geordon countered grimly. "And wolves, and artifacts, and a reputation. Even Gustav would think twice about coming at me when he's outnumbered." He took up his axe from where it leaned against the wall, and brought the returning sphere out of his pocket. "Bar the doors behind me."

Once she'd obliged, and he'd called the wolves to him, Daria watched him from an upper window. He stood on the path in front of the house, scanning the woods with a sharp eye. With the axe propped on his shoulder and the pack of wolves around him, he made quite a formidable figure. He patrolled for hours, sometimes sending a few wolves out scouting further. But after no more sightings of Gustav, Daria began to wonder if the intimidating display had successfully deterred him.

***

When Geordon came back in, he even checked the magic mirror that stood in his room. It indeed showed Gustav passing through the forest—but there was no way to pinpoint where exactly he was, just from the trees visible in the background. Even if Geordon and the wolves went after him, by the time they came across the right location, Gustav would be long gone. In any case, Geordon could tell, based on which side of the trunks was lit by the glow of the setting sun, that Gustav was heading west, back to Nordham. Geordon didn't trust that he wasn't up to anything, but he couldn't watch the mirror every second. He still consulted it each day, though all it displayed was Gustav walking around in town. Maybe he wasn't coming back after all.

~  ~

Geordon sat in a chair by the kitchen wall, sanding a piece of wood to be a new leg for the couch. He looked up when he heard Daria come in.

"All this waiting is making me restless," she sighed. "I feel like taking a walk."

He frowned in concern. "Gustav could still be out there."

"There's been no sign of him in days. And I haven't been out of the house for a week."

Geordon was still reluctant. "All right. But let me have the wolves keep a wide perimeter around you, to make sure he doesn't get anywhere near." He saw her to the front door, and stayed in the threshold, looking out at the forest as he contacted the distant pack. His medallion momentarily glowed a faint silver. When he was done, he looked at Daria again, touching a brief hand to her elbow. "Don't be out too long. It'll be dark soon."

She gave him a slight smile. "Promise."

Geordon watched her walk up the path to the dam until she was out of sight. Then he slowly turned back inside and closed the door. The wolves would alert him if they caught any trace of Gustav, and they'd close ranks around Daria to protect her until Geordon could get there.

As the minutes passed, a thicker cloud cover rolled in, bringing night early. Geordon couldn't focus on his work; a grain of worry was still gnawing at him. *I'll check the mirror again, just to be sure.*

He went up to his bedchamber, and

crossed to the cheval glass. He set his hands on either side of the dark wood frame, activating its magic with the contact, and looked intently into it. "Show me Gustav."

The glass clouded over into a dull grey, then cleared to show a scene in the benighted woods. Gustav stood on a hill above the trees, speaking soundless commands to the man beside him, who was setting up a catapult. With a smirk of grim satisfaction, Gustav turned and pointed out where to aim it. The view shifted to reveal their target in the distance. The great wooden wall of the dam.

Geordon's stomach dropped. If the dam burst, the floodwaters would wash straight for the manor. And Daria was out there. It'd reach her first.

Releasing the mirror, Geordon raced out to find her.

As he charged up the path that led to the dam, Geordon cursed himself. He should've sent a vanguard of wolves with Daria too. He should've checked the mirror first before letting her leave. If anything happened to her...

A wolf stepped out from the trees ahead, yellow eyes glowing faintly in the dark, to see why Geordon was in such a rush, and if he needed any assistance.

"No! Stay away!" Geordon called without stopping, waving a hand for it to go back. "There's a flood coming!"

The wolf turned tail and lolloped back into the woods to warn the rest of the pack—and hopefully some of the other animals, too. One by one, howls rose into the night from all corners of the forest, near and far.

Geordon could have had one of them run ahead to find Daria, and they might have gotten there sooner than he, but he didn't want to send them into the path of danger. She might not have understood them, anyway, and none of them had been closer to her than he already was.

He got an impression from one of the wolves' minds; he'd last seen Daria not long ago, halfway up the hill. Geordon made his legs pump even faster.

A distant boom rumbled through the air. Then another. But it wasn't thunder. Gustav had started bombarding the dam.

Geordon caught sight of Daria ahead. She stood looking around with a slight frown, probably made wary by all the howls. She turned to him as he came running up.

"Gustav's coming tonight," Geordon told her. He caught her hand and started pulling her along with him as he hastened back down the trail. "We must get out of here. He sabotaged the dam."

"What?"

"His plan must be to come for you after he flushes me out with the flood."

"But...that's mad!" she breathed. "It'll fill the whole valley."

Geordon clenched his jaw. "I doubt he cares about that."

A few cold droplets landed on his skin, and soon a light rain began to fall from above.

Daria stared at the ground as they ran. "I'm so sorry," she whispered.

He glanced over at her. "This wasn't your doing."

"But he's doing this because of me," she insisted. "If I hadn't stayed here, I wouldn't have brought this on you."

After a moment, Geordon tightened his hold on her hand. "I wouldn't have had it any other way." Someone like her deserved to have refuge when she needed it. And at least he'd gotten the chance to know her, even for just a short time.

Far behind them, there was a ponderous, groaning *crack* that shook the very earth, followed by a thunderous rushing rumble. Geordon glanced over his shoulder to see a massive torrent of muddy water surging towards them. There was no way they could outrun it now.

He dashed for the side of the path with Daria in tow. He reached for a branch of the nearest tree, intending to climb out of harm's way, or at least hold onto it as a lifeline.

But his hand was still an inch away when the tide rammed into them from the side, bearing them under its freezing waters as it charged downhill. The shock of the impact nearly robbed Geordon of his consciousness. Awash in the churning darkness, he didn't know which way was up—but he still held on tight to Daria's hand, and rowed with his other arm, until his chest burned with the desire to breathe. He fought his way to the surface, pulling Daria up with him, and they each gasped lungfuls of air.

The raging current tossed them about and cascaded over their heads again. Spluttering and struggling to stay afloat, Geordon laboriously drew Daria nearer, cinching his arms around her—though they were starting to go numb from the cold—and holding her close to him. The coursing waves dashed them against tree trunks, but Geordon tried to take the brunt of the impacts with his back, so as to spare Daria. Low branches and driftwood scratched them as they whipped past. Trees were pushed over and even uprooted, and the flood spread out wide through the forest, being added to from above as the rain turned into a downpour.

Finally, the manor came into sight ahead. Beyond it, the rampant river split, one course continuing onward down the steeper slope, the other running past the far side of the house.

As they rapidly neared it, he pushed Daria out from him so she would be caught up in the flow that headed toward the manor. "Get to the house!" he called to her.

"Geordon!" she cried out in anguish as she was swept away from him.

He continued on downhill, far, far along, until the torrent lessened enough that he could try to get his footing on the ground again. He washed up at the lowermost curve of the path, and staggered to his feet. Turning, he made his way around the bend to start climbing up the slope of slick mud. His body ached all over from bruises and scrapes gained during the buffeting, and he walked with a slight limp. He plowed on through the heavy downpour, which plastered his bedraggled hair over his forehead and continued soaking him to the skin. He frequently slipped in the muck, and even fell onto it a few times, sliding several yards back downhill—but he always got back up, eyes fixed on the hilltop ahead, putting one foot in front of the other with dogged perseverance. He would get back to her before Gustav did. Of that, he was determined.

At last, Geordon made it to the crest, and was relieved to see Daria standing on the side porch, an arm around one of the wooden pillars. She must have been able to grab onto it as she coasted by. She was watching anxiously for him, and now discerned his form amidst the darkness.

"Geordon!" she breathed, and rushed down the steps to meet him in the rain. She set a hand on his chest, accompanying him the rest of the way. "Are you all right?"

"If you are." He touched her chin tenderly. There was a nasty abrasion on her cheek, but he hoped he'd been able to shield the rest of her from the worst of it.

Facing forward, he put an arm around her shoulders, but it served more for her to support him than for him to protect her.

They went up the stairs and into the house. A film of water coated the room's floorboards, and was slowly draining through the gaps between them into the cellar. It must have washed in through the cracks under the doors. Geordon set his jaw. This would set back his restoration efforts by months.

The two of them shuffled over to the fireplace and dropped onto the hearthstone before it. Thankfully, the fire was still burning. Slumped with an elbow on his knee, Geordon sank his fingers in his hair, and waited for the heat to dry his clothes. Daria shivered, and huddled closer to the flames. The silence was singularly miserable, with only the drip of droplets from their sopping hair landing on the floor.

The mud on Geordon's clothes began turning to caked dust that he could brush off. The rain outside seemed to be dwindling off.

"He'll be here any minute," he said dully. He lurched to his feet, and helped pull Daria up. They stumbled into the front room, and he went to heft up the thick wooden beam, barring the front double-doors with it. It was only a cursory precaution, since it would make little difference if Gustav thought to look for another way in.

But no sooner had they set foot on the stage than there came a pounding on the door. Geordon turned back to it.

"Take to the cupboard," he told Daria quietly.

She looked at him with alarm. "Geordon..." she murmured.

A man's bellow came through from outside. "I'm here to reclaim what is *mine*, Beast!" The door rattled on its hinges as Gustav started ramming his shoulder against it.

"Leave the door open on your end, so he won't be able to follow you there," Geordon went on to Daria.

"But..." That meant Geordon wouldn't be able to escape to the turret either.

The old beam began to buckle.

"Go," he said again. "I'll hold him off."

Daria climbed up the stack of crates to the cupboard, then got in and teleported in a flash of blue.

The wood bar splintered as the doors burst open.

"Daria!" Gustav called out, storming into the foyer, sword out. "Where have you hidden her, you foul brute?" He cast about, craning his neck to look through the curtained archways into the other dark rooms. "Release her to me!"

Geordon glared at him. "No."

Gustav paused in his tracks, and slowly turned to look back at him with a dark gaze. "No?"

"She does not wish to return with you," Geordon told him. "She has decided to stay here, of her own free will."

"You lie!" Gustav cried. "She would never choose to remain with a creature like you!" He whirled on Geordon, blade at the ready.

"You clearly don't care much for her," Geordon said coldly. "That stunt of yours with the dam could have gravely injured her."

Gustav's face showed a moment of surprise, as if he really hadn't thought of that, but he quickly covered it with indignation.

"You just assumed she would be locked up inside, and I would be the one out hunting, did you?" Geordon clenched his fists. "Not only that, but you caused the destruction of miles of land," he growled. "Did you even stop to think of the ramifications your actions would have on the forest you flooded, and all the creatures that live there?"

Gustav's face hardened. "The fate of the common beasts is none of my concern," he spat. "Typical of you to side with your wild brethren over humankind. There's nothing I wouldn't do for my Daria."

"That's where we differ," Geordon said quietly, a steely glint in his eye. "Daria is not *yours*, nor does she belong to anyone else. And only a weak man would so easily forsake his conscience."

Gustav let out a roar, brandishing his sword. "Enough of this talk! Tell me where she is!" Gustav charged at him, but Geordon leapt nimbly up the stack of crates onto the ledge. "Where is she?" Gustav yelled again.

Geordon stopped beside the leather sword case that leaned upright against the wall. "Somewhere you'll never find her," he said grimly. He opened the latch, stepping back. "Excalibur, go!" he called out, and the sword burst out to sail through the air, pointing straight for Gustav, loyally dedicated to protect its master.

Gustav parried it, but it kept coming at him, swinging and slicing as if wielded by an invisible hand. "What sorcery is this?" he demanded amidst the clangs of steel. "Come out and fight me like a man, you cowardly beast!"

Geordon backed up to the teleportation cupboard and used an arm tucked behind his back to try the door. He tugged on the knob a few times, but it didn't budge. Good. Daria had done as he'd advised.

He crouched down to rummage in a small pile, looking for the returning sphere. It wasn't there. He gritted his teeth. He must have left it on the other side of the gallery. He stood up again.

"Excalibur, you traitor! How could you

fight for the Beast?" Gustav knocked the sword aside, with such force that this time it went flashing across the room to stab into the door of the cupboard right in front of Geordon's face, quivering there for a moment of helpless defeat.

Geordon turned back to Gustav in frustration. "What will it take for you to realize?" he demanded. "I want no part in violence!" He started heading around the side of the colonnade. "I'm not the Beast everyone thinks me to be. I am just a man who wants to be left alone. Your own superstition and fear has built me up into something I'm not." He was about halfway around, now; almost to the artifact...

The teleportation cupboard flashed, and out stepped Daria, holding the orb of levitation and looking around for Geordon.

"No!" Geordon cried out to her. "Get back to safety!"

Gustav barked a derisive laugh. "You hid her in a cupboard?" His tone was saturated with ridicule. "Daria! Fear not! I shall have you rescued from this craven beast in a moment." He faced back to Geordon with a casual flourish of his sword.

But Daria turned to Gustav, squaring her shoulders and setting her expression sternly. "I don't need to be rescued." Gustav looked at her in surprise. "I don't *want* to be rescued. I am under no duress or coercion. Geordon is a good man who took me in when I needed it. I came here, of my own accord, to get away from *you*."

Gustav recoiled as if slapped.

Geordon looked on at Daria with profound admiration.

"He must have bewitched you!" Gustav spluttered.

"He did no such thing." The orb in Daria's palm began to glow an eerie green. She stepped off the ledge, and floated down serenely until her feet touched the floor. Gustav stared at her with wide eyes. "It is entirely my decision to stay here. I won't be returning with you, and I certainly won't be marrying you."

Geordon tossed a grappling rope at one of the columns, then vaulted over the railing and slid down to reach ground level.

Daria started advancing on Gustav, the orb shedding unnatural light on her face. "Now I suggest you leave us in peace."

Geordon moved to keep pace behind Daria, backing her up with his tall presence. He had to fight to keep a properly forbidding face. She was just so impressive.

"If you persist in antagonizing us, we'll be forced to dissuade you by less pleasant means. You don't want to see what else our artifacts can do."

"You've gone mad," Gustav breathed, backing away from her. "You've joined forces with *him!*" Then his face twisted into a mask of scorn. "You never were that much of a catch, anyway. Now I'll have my pick of all the finest women, the ones that are *worthy* of being mine." Whirling, he fled out into the night.

Letting the glow of her orb fade, Daria drifted to a stop and watched him run down the path to town, while Geordon came up beside her.

A howl went up nearby, and Gustav shot a glance over his shoulder as the pack of wolves crested the hill. They charged after him with a series of yips, nipping at his heels.

Daria couldn't help a grin of victory. She turned to Geordon and wrapped her arms about his neck in a hug. He held her close too, one hand on the back of her hair.

"I'm so proud of you," he murmured by her ear.

She backed up to give him a savvy look. "So you admit I'm not the type that needs to be hidden away in an ivory tower?"

Geordon smiled wryly. "No. You're definitely better as a partner in action."

Daria stroked the orb in her hands, harbouring suppressed satisfaction on her face. "So, what's our next step for the restoration efforts?" she prompted.

Geordon quirked the corner of his mouth. "I believe I have an enchanted sponge that should make short work of the flooding in the cellar..."

Together they turned away, sending the door slowly swinging closed behind them. Above the manor, the clouds parted to reveal the white glow of the crescent moon, and in the distance, one of the wolves howled one more time.

The End